The Reluctant Flower Girl

story and pictures by

Lynne Barasch

HarperCollins*Publishers*

The Reluctant Flower Girl
Copyright © 2001 by Lynne Barasch
Printed in Hong Kong. All rights reserved.
www.harperchildrens.com

Library of Congress Cataloging-in-Publication Data
Barasch, Lynne.
The reluctant flower girl / story and pictures by Lynne Barasch.
p. cm.
Summary: Afraid of losing her best friend, a little girl does everything she can to stop her big sister's wedding.
ISBN 0-06-028809-4 — ISBN 0-06-028810-8 (lib. bdg.)
[1. Sisters—Fiction. 2. Weddings—Fiction. 3. Best friends—Fiction. 4. Friendship—Fiction.] I. Title.
PZ7.B22965 Re 2001   [E]—dc21   00-61352
CIP   AC

Typography by Robbin Gourley
1   2   3   4   5   6   7   8   9   10
❖
First Edition

For Julia

My big sister, Annabel, was my best friend. Even though she's a grown-up, we skated together, rode bikes together, and sneaked Mallomars together at night.

Once I brought Annabel to my school for show-and-tell.

And once she brought me to her office to staple papers together.

One day Annabel's
boyfriend, Harold,
came over.

He took Annabel out
on the porch. Then he
kneeled down and popped a
ring out of a box. I heard him ask,
"Will you marry me?" Annabel quickly
said, "Oh yes," and put the ring right on her finger. If
Annabel married Harold, she would move away—away
from me. I would lose my best friend!

It didn't take Annabel and Harold any time to spread the news to
my mother and father. They both hugged Annabel and Harold.
Annabel and Harold hugged each other. No one hugged me.

Finally, Annabel came up to our room. "You'll be my flower girl, April," she promised. "We'll get our dresses together. You can help me choose mine." This was a job I didn't want.

But the try-on session started off pretty well.

"Annabel," I said, "you look like a walking tablecloth!" She could never walk down the aisle in that.

The next dress was even better.

"Now you look like a giant mushroom." I laughed. She couldn't get married in that one, either.

By the third dress, I began to relax.

"You look like a stack of pancakes!" I said. The wedding seemed farther and farther away. But when Annabel appeared next, I didn't say a word.

Annabel looked like a bride.

My dress had a blue sash. Annabel tied a big bow in back. "There's my flower girl," she said. "April, you look like an angel."

But I didn't feel like an angel.

Later that day, I told Harold,
"Annabel snores every night."
Harold smiled.

Then I said, "She wets the
bed, too." He laughed.

"She can't cook a thing!" I
said. Harold said, "Perfect!
I love to cook."

The next night, Harold came over for dinner. When he sat in his chair, he got a very soggy seat from a wet towel I had left there accidentally on purpose.

Next, a big blob of catsup landed on his tie when I helped serve him.

He had to go clean it off. My prize garter snake, Sarah, was waiting
for him in the bathroom sink.

At the wedding rehearsal, I sat next to Harold and tied his shoelaces together when he wasn't looking.

But when it was his turn to stand up, he just sat still and smiled at me.

Then when it was my turn to get up, I fell flat on my face. Harold had tied MY shoelaces together! We both started to laugh. "I won't tell if you won't tell," he whispered.

Before I knew it, the big day came. I wore my dress and sprinkled rose petals down the aisle. Then I stood next to Harold and the best man and waited for Annabel.

Annabel looked so happy. She started walking down the aisle. The
wedding was about to happen!

The best man reached in his pocket for the ring. But it flipped out of his hand, up into the air, and disappeared down the aisle.

Everyone looked, but I was the only one who spotted the ring. At last, here was my chance to stop the wedding.

But Annabel was about to cry. So was Harold, but he clutched
Annabel's hand and tried to comfort her anyway.

I guessed Harold deserved another chance. So I went right to the spot and picked up the ring.

Everyone cheered. Annabel and Harold kissed each other.

And they both kissed me.

When it was all over, Annabel and Harold got in their car and
drove away, just like I knew they would.

I waved and waved until they were just a tiny speck. The wedding
was over. I was all alone.

I went upstairs to my room. It was very quiet.

Just then, I saw a little box on my pillow. I opened the lid.

Inside was the bride and groom from the top of the wedding cake, and a note: